Get Well Soon!

For my parents, for everything – CH

For anyone who is missing someone – MMcQ

GET WELL SOON!
A RED FOX BOOK 978 1 849 41215 5

First published as In a Little While in Great Britain
by The Bodley Head, an imprint of Random House Children's Books

Bodley Head edition published 2005
Red Fox edition published 2007

3 5 7 9 10 8 6 4 2

Set in Bodoni Book

Red Fox Books are published by Random House Children's Books,
61-63 Uxbridge Road, London W5 5SA,
a division of The Random House Group Ltd,
in Australia by Random House Australia (Pty) Ltd,
20 Alfred Street, Milsons Point, Sydney, NSW 2061, Australia,
in New Zealand by Random House New Zealand Ltd,
18 Poland Road, Glenfield, Auckland 10, New Zealand,
in South Africa by Random House (Pty) Ltd,
Isle of Houghton, Corner Boundary Road & Carse O'Gowrie,
Houghton 2198, South Africa,
and in India by Random House India Pvt Ltd,
301 World Trade Tower, Hotel Intercontinental Grand Complex,
Barakhamba Lane, New Delhi 110001, India

THE RANDOM HOUSE GROUP Limited Reg. No. 954009

www.**kidsatrandomhouse**.co.uk

A CIP catalogue record for this book is available from the British Library.

Printed in Singapore

Get Well Soon!

★ Charlotte Hudson

★ *Illustrated by* Mary McQuillan

RED FOX

When Wobbily Fang came down for breakfast, Mummy wasn't there. She wasn't singing with the wolf choir or admiring the view from Snowy Peak. All that was left of her was her moonfeather coat.

“Don’t worry, Wobbily Fang,” said Daddy, ruffling his fur. “Mummy’s not very well and has had to go away for a little while, but we’re going to visit her every day.”

He swung Wobbily Fang into the wagon
and off they went to see her.
Past the pine trees and singing birds,
past the snowy peaks and big rivers
and into a different world.

Mummy lay in a strange room. She didn't look like Mummy. She looked small and lost and alone. Wobbily Fang wanted to give her a hug, but there were too many bottles in the way. Very gently, he reached out for her paw.

“When are you coming home, Mummy?”
he asked.
“In a little while,” said Mummy.

That evening, Wobbily Fang thought about Mummy, far away from the forest and all alone in her strange room.

Then he had an idea. He went down to Bear Hollow and called for the wolf choir.

"I need your help," he told them.

The next morning the wolf choir was waiting for him by the wagon. When they reached the hospital, Wobbily Fang led them into Mummy's room. All at once it was filled with the sounds of forest folk songs.

"How wonderful!" said Mummy,
and her eyes began to sparkle
like they used to. Very gently,
Wobbily Fang reached over
and planted a kiss on the
tip of her nose.

"When are you coming home,
Mummy?" he asked.
"In a little while," said Mummy.

That evening, Wobbily Fang climbed to the top of Snowy Peak.
He took out his paint box and
painted the green pines,
the mountains and
the big blue river.

Under a
blossoming tree
he added two wolves
dancing together.

"How wonderful!" said Mummy when she saw her view from Snowy Peak. Her ears pricked up just like they always did when she was happy.

Wobbily Fang moved the bottles to one side. He climbed onto Mummy's bed and gave her a little hug.

“When are you coming home, Mummy?”
he asked.
“In a little while,” said Mummy.

Wobbily Fang sat in the kitchen that evening. He buried his nose in Mummy's moonfeather coat. It smelled of Mummy and their forest walks to Snowy Peak. Suddenly, a little while seemed an awfully long time.

"What are you going to bring Mummy tomorrow?"
asked Daddy as he tucked Wobbily Fang up in bed.
Wobbily Fang closed his eyes.

There was only one thing left to give.

When they arrived at the hospital the next morning, Wobbily Fang ran up to Mummy's room. But when he got there, her bed was empty!

"Mummy!"

howled Wobbily Fang, but there was no answer.

He snuffled under beds

and opened cupboards,

but it was no good.
Mummy was nowhere
to be found.

And then suddenly,
Wobbily Fang heard the faint
howl of a forest folk song.
He followed it,
down a long corridor . . .

. . . round a corner and there, sitting on a bench
with her suitcase, was Mummy!

Wobbily Fang flew into her arms.
"I've been waiting for you,"
said Mummy, giving him a big hug.
"And you've brought my
moonfeather coat!"

"When are you coming home,
Mummy?" asked Wobbily Fang.

"Now!"
said Mummy.

And off they went.

Also written by
Charlotte Hudson

Dan and Diesel

Who Will Sing My Puff-a-Bye?

Also illustrated by
Mary McQuillan

Dippy's Sleepover, with Jane Clarke

Our Twitchy, with Kes Gray

Shadowhog, with Sandra Horn

Squeaky Clean, with Simon Puttock